牛
Ox

鼠
Rat

虎
Tiger

豬
Pig

兔
Rabbit

狗
Dog

龍
Dragon

For nearly 5,000 years, the Chinese culture has organized time in cycles of twelve years. This Eastern calendar is based upon the movement of the moon (as compared to the Western which follows the sun), and is symbolized by the zodiac circle. An animal that has unique qualities represents each year. Therefore, if you are born in a particular year, then you share the personality of that animal. Now people worldwide celebrate this two-week-long festival in the early spring and enjoy the start of another Chinese New Year.

雞
Rooster

蛇
Snake

猴
Monkey

馬
Horse

羊
Sheep

To my grandparents whose love and labor enabled
a better life for generations to come.
– O.C.

To my family–thank you for your love and support.
Without your selfless sacrifice, this book would not
have been possible. You truly are my greatest blessing.
– J.A.

immedium

Immedium, Inc.   P.O. Box 31846   San Francisco, CA 94131
www.immedium.com

First hardcover edition published 2008.

Edited by Don Menn
Book design by Elaine Chu and Dorothy Mak
Chinese translation by Ling Cho, Grace Mak, and Dorothy Mak
Calligraphy by Lucy Chu

Printed in Malaysia
10 9 8 7 6 5 4 3 2 1

Library of Congress Cataloging-in-Publication Data

Names: Chin, Oliver Clyde, 1969- author. | Alcorn, Miah, illustrator.
Title: The year of the ox : tales from the Chinese zodiac / written by
    Oliver Chin ; illustrated by Miah Alcorn.
Description: San Francisco, CA : Immedium, [2020] | Audience: Ages 3-8. |
    Audience: Grades 2-3. | Summary: Olivia the ox learns what her best
    qualities really are when her friend Mei needs help as a flood threatens
    their village. Lists the birth years and characteristics of individuals
    born in the Chinese Year of the Ox.
Identifiers: LCCN 2020011209 (print) | LCCN 2020011210 (ebook) | ISBN
    9781597021524 (hardcover) | ISBN 9781597021548 (ebook)
Subjects: | CYAC: Oxen--Fiction. | Animals--Infancy--Fiction. | Astrology,
    Chinese--Fiction.
Classification: LCC PZ7.C44235 Ydr 2020 (print) | LCC PZ7.C44235 (ebook)
    | DDC [E]--dc23
LC record available at https://lccn.loc.gov/2020011209
LC ebook record available at https://lccn.loc.gov/2020011210

1-59702-152-0
ISBN 978-1-59702-152-4

The Year of the Ox

·Tales from the Chinese Zodiac·

十二生肖故事系列 牛年的故事

Written by Oliver Chin
Illustrated by Miah Alcorn

文：陈曜豪
图：艾尔康祖曼亚

immedium
Immedium, Inc.
San Francisco. CA

Light glistened off the morning dew, and the rising sun welcomed another day. Inside the stables, Mama and Papa Ox yawned after a long night. Resting in their bed of hay, they tickled their new baby.

旭日初升，露珠闪耀着光芒，朝阳又迎来了新的一天。 经过漫漫长夜，
牛爸爸和牛妈妈在牛棚里打了个呵欠，他们躺在干草床上，搔弄着他们的初生宝宝。

Mama smiled,
"Hello there, honey."
Only a few hours old,
the youngster
was rustling
about already.

She had a sweet
and peaceful manner,
so Papa suggested,
"Let's call her Olivia."

牛妈妈微笑地逗说：
"嗨，蜜糖儿！"
虽然只出生几小时，
这个初生之犊已经很活跃好动。

她的个性既可爱又平和，
牛爸爸于是提议，
"让我们叫她奥利维亚吧。"

The proud parents introduced the calf to their friends. "She'll be a big gal!" they all agreed.

Mama whispered, "Tomorrow you'll meet the farmer's daughter. Her name is Mei."

自豪的父母向他们的朋友介绍自己的牛宝宝，"她将会是一个高大的女孩！"朋友們都贊同。

牛妈妈轻声说："明天妳就会遇见农夫的女儿，她的名字叫做美。"

During her first visit, the girl petted Olivia and combed her hair. "I know we'll be best friends," smiled Mei, and she adopted Olivia as her little sister.

The grateful heifer promised, **"I'll always look out for you!"**

初次见面，农夫的女儿抚摸奥利维亚及梳理她的毛发，
美又笑着说："我知道我们会成为最好的朋友。"
她还把奥利维亚认作妹妹。

小母牛感激地答应道：
"我会一直照顧妳！"

Sharing a bubbly spirit, the girls played tag,
"Hide and Seek," and "Kick the Can."

In the countryside, the pair loved to stop and smell the roses.
But sometimes their wild wandering would make quite a mess.

在分享欢乐的时光中，她們玩追逐遊戲，玩捉迷藏和踢罐子。

在农村，这对活宝贝喜欢停下来嗅嗅玫瑰的芬芳，
但有时她们的野外逛游也会弄到一身脏。

Afterwards, Olivia's parents took her aside. Mama noted, "There's a time and place for fun and games."

Papa added, "Yes, dear – it's about time you learned to pull your own weight around here."

之后，奥利维亚的父母拉她到一旁。牛妈妈告诉她，
"是時候分配玩樂的時間和地點。"

牛爸爸也附着说："对，亲爱的，
现在差不多是尽妳本份的时候了。"

The following morning, Papa and Mama showed her the shed where they got ready for work. Every day the bull and cow would each carry a yoke and pull a plow.

翌日早上，牛爸爸和牛妈妈带着她去看看他们准备工作的棚子。
牛爸爸和牛妈妈每天都各自带着颈轭和拉动耕犁辛勤工作。

Olivia wanted to pitch in, despite Mama's misgivings. Papa pointed out, "But the yoke is heavy and tilling the ground is hard labor."

Olivia boasted, **"I'm a big girl now, and I can handle it by myself."**

尽管牛妈妈心存疑虑，奥利维亚仍然很想要投入工作，
牛爸爸指出，"负着颈轭已经很沉重，耕耘起来更是很费力的工夫呢。"

奥利维亚自负地说："我现在是个大女孩了，
我可以處理好自己的事。"

But try as she might, Olivia was too small to plow the fields. Many times she got stuck in the mud and had to be rescued, **"Mooo!"**

After a long day, Olivia came home dirty and plum tuckered out.

尽管倾尽全力，奥利维亚到底是太幼小了，
所以她多次在泥田里堵住了，需要营救地喊："哞！"

经过漫长的一天工作，
奥利维亚弄到又脏又累地回家。

After dinner Mama advised, "Dear, maybe you could try a different job."

"Yes, I'd like that very much," answered Olivia eagerly.

吃过晚餐，牛妈妈建议，"亲爱的，妳或许可以换过别的工作。"

"好喔，我喜欢这提议，"奥利维亚急切地回答。

The next day, Mei led Olivia to the nearby well to fetch some water. Gingerly the girl filled her bucket and balanced it upon her head.

Her little sister bragged,
"Ha, I can carry much more than you!"

第二天，美帶著奥利维亚一起到附近的水井打水。美小心翼翼地把水桶装满，并平衡地顶在头上。

她的小妹妹夸耀说："哈，我可以提水比妳更多。"

"Be careful!" Mei warned as Olivia moseyed along with two buckets on her shoulders. They were almost home when a rooster bumped into them and crowed! Olivia slipped and spilled the water everywhere.

美看到奥利维亚两肩提着两桶水慢步而行，不禁提醒她，"小心！"当她们即将返到家时，一只公鸡撞向她们并咯咯啼！奥利维亚因此滑倒并把水桶打翻，使井水泻满一地。

After cleaning up, Mei thought of another chore for Olivia: "Next week is harvest time. You could bring the rice to be milled." Olivia nodded, and they prepared to collect the crop.

清理后，美为奥利维亚安排另一项工作说：
"下周是收成的時候，你可以带着米去磨。"
奥利维亚点点头，接着她们便准备
去收割庄稼。

During the harvest, Mei loaded stalks of grain onto Olivia's back. **"This is easy,"** smirked Olivia.

But on the way to the mill, a snake darted in front her. Startled, Olivia scattered her load all over the road!

在收割时候，美把谷物堆放在奥利维亚的背上。
"很容易的工夫！"奥利维亚傻傻地笑说。

但在往磨坊路上，一条蛇飞奔到她前面，
奥利维亚吓了一惊，
把背上谷物散跌在路上！

Now both girls were embarrassed. But the weekend
was here, and Mei's parents had planned to sell their
vegetables at the local farmers market. Olivia promised
to behave, so Mama and Papa let her come too.

现在女孩們都感到很过意不去。
但周末已至，美的父母已计划带着他们的蔬菜到当地的农夫市场出售。
奥利维亚答应会乖乖的，所以牛爸爸牛妈妈也就让她一起去。

The town square bustled with buying and selling, and Mei's parents displayed their bounty.

Olivia marveled at all the sights, sounds, and smells. Meeting a friendly rat, she followed it to a stall close by.

市集广场充满了买卖的喧闹，美的父母摆好他们的货物待售。

奥利维亚对在市集所见到、听到和嗅到的一切都啧啧称奇，她还结识了一位老鼠朋友，并跟着去到附近的一个摊子。

Suddenly a yell rang out, "Eeeek!" Soon a crowd had gathered...
to watch Olivia eat someone's fruit! Neighbors wagged their hooves,
Papa shook his horns, and Mei hurried to drag her pal away.

突然大喊一声："咿！"不久一班群众聚集⋯
望着奥利维亚吃别人的水果！邻近的群众在摆动蹄足，
牛爸爸摇摆他的头角，美则连忙跑过去把她拉走。

After the commotion subsided, Mama moaned,
"Darling, I guess you're not old enough to help us after all."
Mei and her parents were disappointed too. So Olivia
trudged back with her tail between her legs.

在骚动平息之后，牛妈妈呻吟著，
"小宝贝，我想你仍未长大到可以帮助我们呢。"
美和她的父母也很失望，
所以奥利维亚唯有垂头丧气地回去。

At home, Olivia wanted to prove she was a hard worker. But Mei's parents had business in town with Mama and Papa. Leaving to tend the fields, Mei told Olivia, "Please just stay behind and out of trouble."

在家里，奥利维亚想证明她是个勤奋工作的牛，
但美的父母及牛爸爸和牛妈妈在镇上正忙碌中。
而美出门往田间工作前，对奥利维亚说：
"請好好留在家中，不要再惹事端啊。"

Alone with little to do, Olivia vowed,
"I'll show them, somehow."

独自留在家里没事干，奥利维亚发誓说：
"无论如何，我要证明给他们看。"

Later she heard a cry pierce the sky, "Waaah!"

过了一会儿，她听到画破天空的叫声:"哗!"

As noises suddenly filled the air,
Olivia rushed outside
and couldn't believe her eyes.

突然四周弥漫了声浪，
奥利维亚迅速跑出屋外，
她简直不敢相信所看见的一切。

Everyone was running away from the farmland that was quickly flooding. The old dam had burst!

"Mooo!" bellowed Olivia, but no one stopped to help. Immediately she wondered, **"Where is Mei?"**

每个人都从瞬间就被洪水
淹没的耕地裏逃跑着，
旧水坝崩堤了！

"哞!"奥利维亚也在叫嚷，
但没有一个停下来去帮助救援。
跟着她立即想知道，"美在何处呢？"

Olivia jumped into the rice paddy to search for her sister.
Passersby warned her, "Leave while you can!"

But she pressed on against the current and finally spotted Mei
clinging to the branches of a cypress tree.

奥利维亚跳入水浸的禾田里寻找她的姊姊。
过路的都警告她说:"走得你便要走了!"

她坚持着逆流而上继续寻找,
她终于看到美吊挂在柏树的树枝上。

Wet and worried, Mei was
surprised to see Olivia,
"What are you doing here?"

"This is no time for questions,"
Olivia sputtered.
"Get down and climb on board!"

美又湿又担心之际，
意外地见到奥利维亚，
她问："你在这里干嘛？"

奥利维亚急得口沫四溅的答道：
"没有时间答问了，
快些下来爬在我的背上逃生吧！"

Swimming towards home, Olivia picked up others stranded by the rising water. Juggling them on her shoulders, Olivia plowed ahead. At last, she clambered over the ridge to safety.

向着家游回去时，沿途并救起被洪水围困的其他动物。
奥利维亚把他们扛在肩上，就好像犁田般把动物拖回去。
最后她攀到山脊，找到安全的地方。

But before they could catch their breath,
they noticed the bank had begun to buckle.
If it gave way, the water would flood
the village below.

Mei cried, "We need to warn
the townsfolk!"

但当他们还没有喘过气来，
她们发觉河床已开始弯曲。
万一河床决堤，
河水会淹没下游的村庄。

美大叫起来：
"我们一定要警告村民啊！"

"**Hurry up and go!**" replied Olivia, as she pressed her shoulder against the dike. "**I'll hold it up.**"

Hesitating, Mei hopped on her bicycle. "I'll pedal as fast as I can, and you'd better still be here when I come back!"

"快些去吧！"奥利维亚同时又把她的
肩膀抵着堤坝说："我会撑着它的。"

犹豫了一会，美跳上她的脚踏车，
"我会尽最快速度踩著踏板去通知大家，
当我回来时，你一定仍然要在这里呀！"

Leaning against the crumbling wall, Olivia spotted a crack where water began dripping through.

奥利维亚背撑着快要崩塌的墙壁时，又侦察到一条裂缝，水滴正开始渗漏出来。

She needed to patch it, but didn't dare move. What could she do?

她要去堵住裂口，但又不敢移动。她要怎办呢？

Hastily she stuck her tail into the hole!

匆忙中只有用她的尾巴塞进裂口里！

The plug held, and Olivia sighed in relief.
Feeling the world's weight on her shoulders,
Olivia didn't want to let everybody down.
Digging her hooves into the ground,
she pushed with all her might.

"MOOOOOO!!"

裂口堵住了，
这时奥利维亚才松一口气。
觉得全世界的重担都压在她的
肩膀上，奥利维亚不想令人失望。
所以她用尽全力去撑着河堤，直到她的
足蹄都钻在泥地里，她仍奋力地撑喊着"哞!!"

Time crawled by. Just then Mei's family and
Mama and Papa arrived with lots of helpers.

As the waters finally receded,
Olivia took a break. She was dirty, soggy,
and hungry, but was very happy.

时间慢慢过去，终于等到美的家人和
牛爸妈一起带着人来帮忙。

最后河水退掉，奥利维亚可以休息一下，
她虽然又脏、又湿、又饿，但她却非常开心。

Mei hugged Olivia, "Thanks for coming back for me."
Olivia blushed, **"I know you'd do the same."**

Joyfully Mama and Papa remarked,
"You two are the bravest girls
in the whole world."

美拥抱着奥利维亚说:"谢谢你跑回来救我。"
奥利维亚红着脸说:"我知道你也会一样这么做的。"

高兴的牛爸爸牛妈妈表示,"妳俩是全世界最勇敢的女孩。"

Soon life returned to normal, and Olivia and Mei played their games and roamed about as before. Their parents watched how they were growing up, both hungry for adventure and strong-willed.

不久之后，生活一切回复如常，奥利维亚和美好像从前一样，
玩她们爱玩的游戏和想去的地方。 她们的父母看着她们成长的过程，
她俩都渴望探索新事物和培养到坚强的意志。

These sisters loved each other heart and soul.
Mei knew that Olivia was there for her when it counted.
And everyone around would remember that
this was a marvelous Year of the Ox.

这对小姊妹全心全意地彼此相爱，
美知道在重要的时候奥利维亚会在她身边。
周围的人都会记得那是一个奇妙的牛年。

牛

Ox
1925, 1937, 1949, 1961, 1973, 1985, 1997, 2009, 2021, 2033

People born in the Year of the Ox are patient, stout, and down-to-earth.
They are plain-spoken and hard-working. But sometimes they can be creatures of
habit – cautious and headstrong. Though they may be slow to rouse, oxen are
dependable characters indeed.

在牛年出生的人有耐性，健硕，实事求是。 他们直言不讳和做事用功。但有时他们是习性
小心和倔强的动物。 虽然他们可能会慢热一点，但属牛的人的性格是绝对可以信赖！

Learn about
cool inventions
from Asia!

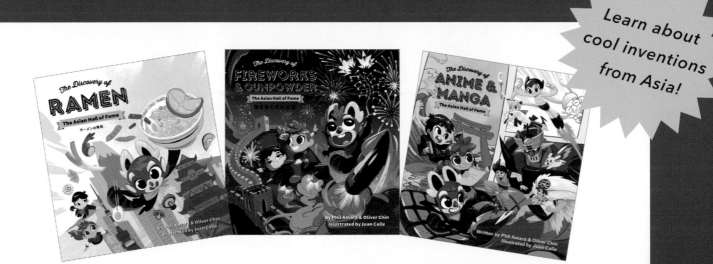

"Whatever your age, *The Discovery of Ramen* is an experience to whet
your appetite with a subject worth savoring."- *Sampan*

"[*Fireworks & Gunpowder* has] a simple yet brilliantly explained set of facts
worked into the story, and some really gorgeous illustrations" –Read it Daddy

"An appealing, informative read for anime and manga enthusiasts
that shows young fans that their favorite comic and animation style has
a long and rich history." - *School Library Journal*